Weekly Reader Presents

Waggleby of Fraggle Rock

By Stephanie Calmenson
Pictures by Barbara McClintock

Muppet Press
Henry Holt and Company
NEW YORK

Copyright © 1985 by Henson Associates, Inc.
Fraggle Rock, Fraggles, Muppets, and character names are trademarks of Henson Associates, Inc.
All rights reserved, including the right to reproduce this
book or portions thereof in any form.
Published by Henry Holt and Company,
521 Fifth Avenue, New York, New York 10175

Library of Congress Cataloging in Publication Data

Calmenson, Stephanie.
Waggleby of Fraggle Rock.
Summary: Boober befriends a cave creature with some
very distinctive habits—and some lovable ones too.
1. Children's stories, American.   [1. Puppets—
Fiction]   I. McClintock, Barbara, ill.   II. Title.
PZ7.C136Wag   1985   [E]   84-16599

ISBN: 0-03-003259-8

Printed in the United States of America

LAUNDRY. That is what Boober Fraggle loves to do when he's
not sitting around thinking about germs, falling rocks, and
the end of the world. Boober, you see, is a worrier.

   He does not know it yet, but just inside his laundry basket
is a brand-new worry. . . .

"One blue sock, another blue sock. One brown sock,
another brown sock. One yellow ear . . . YELLOW EAR?"
cried Boober. "Yipes!!"

Boober did not wait around to find out what he had just hung up on his clothesline. "Help!" he shouted, running to the Great Hall to sound the alarm.

In an instant, thousands of Fraggles had gathered round.
Boober's closest friends—Gobo, Wembley, Mokey, and
Red—made their way to the front of the crowd.
"What's the matter?" asked Mokey.

"Doom . . . gloom . . . yellow ears!" Boober was so excited he couldn't even talk straight.

"Boober, take it easy. What has yellow ears?" asked Red.

"*Laundry . . . hanging . . . yellow ears!*" Boober shouted.

"You'd better show us what you're talking about," said Gobo.

Boober led his four friends back to his cave. Gobo, the bravest, went in first.

"It's a cave creature!" said Gobo.

"What's a cave creature doing here?!" moaned Boober.

"It's come to visit you," said Mokey. "And cave creatures don't visit just anyone. You should be honored."

"He sure likes you," added Red. "Look at his tail wagging."

Thump, thump, thump.

"Why don't you give him a name?" said Mokey.

"I don't want to give him a name," said Boober. "I don't even want to let him stay!"

The cave creature licked Boober's face adoringly.

"Yecch!" said Boober. "Wetness and germs!"

Thump, thump, thump.

"There goes that tail again," said Gobo. "Maybe you should call him Wags."

"Or Wagger," suggested Red.

"How about Waggleby?" Mokey said. "It's got a nice ring to it."

"Sounds good to me," said Wembley.

"Let's leave Boober and Waggleby alone so they can get to know each other better," suggested Gobo.

"Wait!" Boober begged. "Don't go!"

But it was too late.

"*Swoof! Swoof!*" barked Waggleby as he began to explore the cave. First he found Boober's collection of lucky stones. He left no stone unturned.

Then he went for Boober's hats.

"Oh no! Not my hats!" Boober cried.

Waggleby chewed through Boober's red beret, his green fedora, and his bright blue beanie.

But when Waggleby tugged Boober's freshly washed and best-loved scarf from the line, Boober had to take action.

"GIVE ME MY SCARF!" he shouted.
He grabbed the scarf and pulled and pulled. Waggleby
thought this was great fun, until...

. . . Boober's scarf tore right down the middle. Boober and Waggleby went flying.

While Boober was digging out of the mess, Waggleby went to find something to eat. He followed his nose to a freshly baked carrot loaf, a dish of radish soufflé, and a specially seasoned stew that Boober was saving for dinner. The special seasoning in the stew came from a flava flower. Flava flowers, which are very hard to find, make food irresistible to Fraggles.

The flowers were what Waggleby spotted next.

He was just finishing the last one when Boober found him.
"That does it!" Boober yelled. "It took me weeks to find those flowers! Out! Get out of here!"

Waggleby's tail dropped to the floor with a thud. Then slowly, he left the cave.

"I'm glad Waggleby's gone, I am!" said Boober. "He's noisy, nosy, germy, and he makes a mess of everything." Boober looked at his empty flower jar. "How will I ever find another flava flower? They bloom once every three years!" Boober picked up his laundry and began to wash it furiously.

He felt better when he had finished, and went to mix up a batch of radish rolls. "That cave creature had better not darken my doorstep again, if he knows what's good for him," Boober muttered.

The next thing Boober knew,
he was up in the air...

...then down on the floor.

Boober ran to see what had happened.
A rumbling noise was coming from the
Cave of Three Corners.

"Great Gorgs of fire!" yelled Boober when he got there.

A huge pile of rocks blocked the entrance to the cave. Sticking out at the bottom was the tip of a yellow tail.

It figures, thought Boober.

Thump, thump, went the tail weakly.

For a moment, Boober considered leaving Waggleby there. Then he thought better of it, and began to unpile the rocks one by one.

"*Swoof! Swoof!*" barked Waggleby when he was free.
He dropped a flava flower at Boober's feet.

Boober could hardly believe it. Waggleby had found
another flava flower!

Boober carefully picked up the flower and took it back to his cave. He put it in the jar of water. Instantly, more flowers grew.

"Ah," said Boober. "Once again my amazingly delicious dishes will become truly incredible!"

Boober mixed three flower petals in with some radish jam. Then he spread the jam on the warm rolls he had just baked.

As if by magic, Gobo, Wembley, Mokey, and Red appeared.

"What is that magnificent aroma, Boober?" asked Mokey.

"Oh, just a little something I threw together," answered Boober.

"These are great," said Red, as she finished her seventh roll
with jam.

"*Swoof, swoof!*" barked Waggleby.

"Why don't you ask Waggleby in to have some?" Mokey
said. "He sounds hungry."

Boober jumped up to guard the door.

"Absolutely, positively, most very definitely . . ."

"*Swoof, swoof,*" Waggleby barked as sweetly as he knew how. Boober ignored him.

"As I was saying," Boober continued, "absolutely, positively, most very definitely *no.*"

"*Swoof, swoof,*" Waggleby tried again.

"Oh, come on, Boober," said Red.

"*Never!*" said Boober. "Waggleby is the most impossible creature I have ever met!"

Then he remembered the flower that Waggleby had given to him. He stopped to think.

It was a difficult decision. Finally, Boober made up his mind.

"Listen, Waggleby," Boober said. "If you try not to be noisy, and try not to be nosy, and try not to be germy, and try not to make a mess of everything, then . . ."

Waggleby was inside eating warm rolls with jam in the
time it takes to say "five Fraggle friends."
Thump, thump, thump!